The HAUNTED LIBRARY

FOR BEN
—DHB

* * * * * * * * * * * * * * * * * *

I'd like to thank my agent, Sara Crowe, and everyone at Grosset & Dunlap for all their hard work on my behalf; also my long-time critique group, Delia Howard, Jennifer Reinhardt, and Tess Weaver, for their willingness to read and comment on an entire book with very little notice; Kellye Carter Crocker for insisting I make her a promise (without that promise, this series might never have come to be); the Coralville Public Library for giving me a place to write, and the Nano Rebels for the years of friendship and camaraderie. We can always make new friends, but we can't make new old friends.

* * * * * * * * * * * * * * * * * *

GROSSET & DUNLAP
Published by the Penguin Group
Penguin Group (USA) LLC, 375 Hudson Street, New York, New York 10014, USA

USA | Canada | UK | Ireland | Australia | New Zealand | India | South Africa | China

penguin.com
A Penguin Random House Company

Text copyright © 2014 by Dori Hillestad Butler. Illustrations copyright © 2014 by Aurore Damant. All rights reserved. Published by Grosset & Dunlap, a division of Penguin Young Readers Group, 345 Hudson Street, New York, New York 10014. GROSSET & DUNLAP is a trademark of Penguin Group (USA) LLC. Printed in the USA.

Library of Congress Cataloging-in-Publication Data is available.

ISBN 978-0-448-46244-8 (pbk)   10 9 8 7 6 5 4 3 2
ISBN 978-0-448-46245-5 (hc)   10 9 8 7 6 5 4 3 2 1

The HAUNTED LIBRARY

THE GHOST IN THE ATTIC

BY DORI HILLESTAD BUTLER
ILLUSTRATED BY AURORE DAMANT

GROSSET & DUNLAP ✶ AN IMPRINT OF PENGUIN GROUP (USA) LLC

GHOSTLY GLOSSARY

EXPAND
When ghosts make themselves larger

GLOW
What ghosts do so humans can see them

HAUNT
Where ghosts live

PASS THROUGH
When ghosts travel through walls,
doors, and other solid objects

SHRINK
When ghosts make themselves smaller

SKIZZY
When ghosts feel sick to their stomachs

SOLIDS
What ghosts call humans, animals,
and objects they can't see through

SPEW
What comes out when ghosts throw up

SWIM
When ghosts move freely through the air

WAIL
What ghosts do so humans can hear them

CHAPTER 1

YES, WE DO HAUNTED HOUSES

W hat's the matter, Kaz?" Claire asked as she shook the dice in her hand. "You look so sad."

Kaz *was* sad. He and Claire were playing a dice game in the craft room. Claire rolled the dice for both of them. Kaz couldn't help noticing that Claire always seemed to roll better for herself than she did for him.

But that wasn't why Kaz was sad. He was sad because it had been three weeks

since he'd lost his haunt. And three weeks since he'd seen his mom, his dad, his brother Little John, or his dog, Cosmo.

It had been even longer than that since he'd seen his brother Finn, or his grandparents.

Mom and Dad always said that maybe one day Finn, Grandmom, and Grandpop would find their way back to their old haunt. But Kaz knew that would never happen now.

Their haunt was gone. And his entire family was gone, too. The wind had carried Kaz over fields . . . houses . . . trees . . . and into Claire's library. Kaz had no idea what had happened to the rest of his family. Or if he'd ever see them again.

"Are you thinking about your family?" Claire asked.

"Sort of," Kaz admitted.

Claire was a solid, but she wasn't like other solids. She could see ghosts when they weren't glowing. And she could hear ghosts when they weren't wailing.

Kaz was a ghost, but he wasn't like other ghosts. He couldn't glow. He couldn't wail. And he didn't like to pass through solid objects.

"Don't worry, Kaz," Claire said. "We'll find your family. That's why we started our detective agency, remember?"

Beckett snickered. He was the other ghost who lived at the library. Beckett spent most of his time in his secret room behind the bookcase in the craft room. But sometimes he came out to read library books.

"What?" Claire narrowed her eyes at Beckett. "What are you laughing at?"

"Nothing," Beckett said, turning

a page in a book. "If you want to call yourselves detectives, it isn't any of my business. But you've only solved one case, and it wasn't even a hard one."

"It was, too!" Claire argued.

Kaz had to agree. He had thought he and Claire would never figure out who, or what, was haunting the library.

"If you say so," Beckett said. "But let me ask you this: Who's going to hire a kid and a ghost to solve a mystery?"

"People who have ghosts in their houses," Claire said, like it was obvious.

Beckett snickered again.

"We won't laugh at them like grown-up detectives would," Claire said. "We'll go to their houses and find their ghosts. And even if those ghosts don't want to talk to me, they'll talk to Kaz. Because he's a ghost like they are."

"How is Kaz going to go anywhere?" Beckett asked. "He can't go into the Outside. He'll blow away."

Kaz hadn't thought about that.

But Claire shrugged like it was no big deal. "We'll figure something out."

"How will those solids—" Beckett began.

"Don't call us solids," Claire interrupted. Kaz knew Claire didn't like that word.

But that didn't stop Beckett. "How will those *solids*"—he put extra emphasis on the word "solids" just to annoy Claire—"find out about your detective agency? Will you put an ad in the newspaper? Will you hang a sign on the door? What about your parents? Do they know about your detective agency?"

Kaz doubted that. Claire's parents

thought she was too young to be a detective.

"What would your parents say if they knew you'd started a detective agency?" Beckett asked. "Maybe I should show myself and tell them."

"You better not." Claire leaped to her feet. "Why don't you go back behind your wall and leave us alone?"

"Claire?" called a voice behind them.

Kaz turned to see Claire's grandma, Grandma Karen. She was the librarian, and she lived above the library with Claire and Claire's parents. Grandma Karen also took care of Claire when Claire's parents were away solving mysteries.

"Who are you talking to, dear?" Grandma Karen asked, patting the pink stripe in her hair.

Claire's grandma was the only person,

ghost or solid, Kaz had ever seen with hair like that.

"No one," Claire said, biting her lip.

Grandma Karen stepped into the room and looked around. She couldn't see Kaz or Beckett, not even when they floated right in front of her.

"Well, your parents would like to speak to you," Grandma Karen said. "They're upstairs in their office."

"Okay," Claire said, reaching for her green bag. That bag was where she kept all her detective supplies. She never went anywhere without it.

Kaz followed Claire up the stairs. They found Claire's dad standing in the hallway, tapping his foot. There were two suitcases on the floor beside him.

Claire's mom was in their office talking into a thing called a phone or a telephone. Kaz wasn't sure which was the right word. Whatever it was, he loved watching solids talk into those things. It was so interesting that solids could talk to other solids who weren't actually there.

"No, I'm sorry," Claire's mom said

into the telephone. "That's not the kind of work we do." She touched a button on her phone and set it down on the desk.

"Who was that?" Claire's dad asked.

"Just another crazy person who thinks she has a ghost in her attic." Claire's mom rolled her eyes.

Ghost? Kaz and Claire glanced at each other.

"We don't have time for such nonsense," Dad said. "We'll miss our flight."

Claire cleared her throat. "Grandma said you wanted to see me?"

"Oh yes, Claire," her mom said as she stacked some papers together on her desk. "We wanted to tell you that we have to go out of town for a few days."

"Again?" Claire asked.

"I'm afraid so," Mom said. "It's business, honey. There's nothing we can do about it."

"Help your grandma while we're gone," Dad said, ruffling her hair.

"And don't bother her with ghost talk," Mom said. Claire's parents didn't believe that she could see ghosts, and they didn't like it when she said she could. They were afraid people would think she was strange.

They hugged her good-bye, picked up their suitcases, and left.

As soon as they were gone, Claire went to her mom's desk and picked up the telephone.

"What are you doing?" Kaz asked.

"I'm going to call the 'crazy person' back and see if she'll hire us to come find her ghost."

Claire pushed some buttons on the phone, then held it to her ear. "Hello," she said. "My name is Claire Kendall. You just called By the Books Detectives." She paused. "No, they don't handle ghosts. But C & K *Ghost* Detectives does."

Claire listened for a while, then reached for a pen and pad of paper. "Can I get your name and address?"

Kaz watched her write: VICTORIA BEESLEY. 315 FOREST STREET.

"Okay, Mrs. Beesley. I'll be right there." Claire set the phone on the desk and grinned at Kaz. "We've got a case! A real ghost case!"

There was only one problem: Kaz couldn't go with Claire. Like Beckett said, if he went into the Outside, he would blow away.

CHAPTER 2

HOW TO TRAVEL SAFELY OUTSIDE

have an idea," Claire said. "You can shrink, right?"

"Yes," Kaz said. Shrinking was one ghost skill he had mastered. But he didn't understand how that would help. It didn't matter whether he expanded, shrank, or stayed his normal size. If he went into the Outside, the wind would blow him away.

"Follow me," Claire said.

Kaz swam after her. When they got

to the kitchen, Claire opened a cabinet and took out a tall, rounded container with green stars on it. "This is my water bottle. Can you shrink small enough to fit inside?"

Kaz looked at it. "Sure," he said. He used to shrink much smaller than that whenever he played Keep Away with his brothers back at their old haunt.

"Good," Claire said. "Because if you can ride in here, then I can take you with me anywhere."

"Even into the Outside?" Kaz asked.

"Even outside."

"And I won't blow away?"

"I don't think so," Claire said.

I don't think so was not the same as *No, you won't*. But Kaz was willing to give the bottle a try. He took a deep breath and shrank down . . . down . . .

down . . . until he was no larger than Claire's finger. Then he spun around three times and swam into the bottle.

"That is so cool," Claire said. She always said that when Kaz shrank. Shrinking wasn't something solids could do. Not even if they tried really, really hard.

Claire peered in at Kaz through the open top. Her eyes and nose now looked *huge* to Kaz. "How is it?" Claire asked. "Do you have enough room in there?"

Kaz swam in a circle all around the bottle. He had plenty of room. And even if he didn't, he could shrink a little smaller.

It was kind of hard to see out through the side of the bottle, though, because there were green stars all over it.

"It's fine," he said, floating between the stars.

"Okay," Claire said. "I'm going to put the top on the bottle now."

Kaz ducked as a green lid came down over the top of the bottle.

"Can you still hear me with the top on?" Claire asked. Her voice sounded a

little muffled, but Kaz could hear her.

"Yes. Can you hear me?" he asked.

"Yes," Claire said. She picked up the bottle with Kaz inside and looped the strap over her shoulder. "Let's go!"

The bottle swung back and forth against Claire's hip as she skipped down the stairs.

Kaz felt both excited and a little bit nervous. He was going into the Outside! With Claire!

"Grandma?" Claire called, her hand on the front door. "I'm going for a walk, okay?"

Grandma Karen poked her head into the entryway. "By yourself?" she asked.

Claire hugged the bottle with Kaz inside close to her body. "Yes," she said.

"Well, I'm glad you're finally getting some fresh air," Grandma Karen said.

"Maybe you'll even find a new friend?"

"Maybe," Claire said.

"Please be home by four o'clock," Grandma Karen said.

Claire opened the door and stepped into the Outside.

Brightness! That was the first thing Kaz noticed about the Outside. Everything was so bright.

But he felt reasonably safe traveling inside Claire's bottle. He was even starting to enjoy the Outside a little bit. It was so full of color.

As Claire walked, Kaz saw gray sidewalk and green grass below him . . . blue sky with white fluffy clouds above him . . . trees with bright green leaves and dark red leaves to his right . . . flowers in every color of the rainbow to his left.

He heard birds chirping . . . insects buzzing . . . wind rustling through the leaves . . . and in the distance he heard a familiar "Woof! Woof!"

Kaz turned toward the sound. It almost sounded like his dog, Cosmo. But it couldn't be.

Could it?

Kaz peered between two green stars.

He didn't see any dogs, ghost or solid.

"How long will it take to get where we're going?" Kaz asked.

"Not long," Claire said as she turned a corner. This was a busier street than the last one they'd been on. Cars and trucks whizzed past. Kaz had never been so close to cars and trucks before.

"Woof! Woof!"

Kaz whirled around. This time he caught a glimpse of a white tail before it disappeared into a bush. A white *ghost* tail that looked exactly like Cosmo's.

"Cosmo?" Kaz cried, swimming all around the bottle in search of a better view. "Cosmo? Is that you?"

"Who's Cosmo?" Claire asked. She held her water bottle up so she and Kaz were at eye level. "Is that your dog? Do you see him somewhere?"

"I don't know," Kaz said. "I heard him first. At least I think I did. Then I thought I saw him go into that bush over there." He pointed.

"Let's go see." Claire skipped over to the bush.

She set the bottle and her detective bag on the grass, then got down on her hands and knees and peered under the

bush. Kaz tried to look, too, but he couldn't see through Claire's solid body.

"I don't see anything," Claire said. She stood up and walked all around the bush.

But no ghost dogs or solid dogs appeared.

"Maybe it was my imagination," Kaz said glumly.

"Well, the good news is that we're on Forest Street," Claire said, pointing up at a sign. "And look: There's 315, right across the street."

Claire grabbed the bottle and her bag and hurried across the street.

"When we get inside, I'll let you out of the bottle," Claire told Kaz. "While I'm talking to the lady who lives here, you fly around her house and see if you can find the ghost."

"Okay," Kaz said, even though ghosts don't really fly. They swim.

He could hardly wait to find out who was haunting this house. Was it his mom? His dad? Little John? Finn? His grandparents? Or a ghost who wasn't even in his family?

CHAPTER 3

MRS. BEESLEY'S CLOSET

I wouldn't knock on that door if I were you," called a voice from next door.

Kaz and Claire looked over and saw a redheaded boy about their age. He held an orange ball in the crook of his arm and watched Claire curiously. Kaz was pretty sure the boy couldn't see him.

Claire walked over to the edge of the porch. "Why not?" she asked, leaning on the railing.

"Because the lady who lives in that

house is weird," the boy said. "She's been telling the whole neighborhood that her house is haunted."

"I'm not afraid of weird people or haunted houses," Claire said.

The boy shrugged. "Don't say I didn't warn you," he said. He turned and bounced his ball on the driveway.

Claire went over to the door and knocked crisply three times.

A lady around Grandma Karen's age came to the door. She wore a purple housedress and a yellow band with a flower in her hair. "Yes?" she said, peering down at Claire.

"Hello," Claire said cheerfully. "Are you Mrs. Beesley? I'm Claire Kendall. I'm here to find your ghost."

Mrs. Beesley tilted her glasses to get a better look at Claire. "*You're* the detective?"

"Yes," Claire said.

"Aren't you a little young to be a detective?"

"No." Claire stood up a little taller. "I'm older than I look. Plus, sometimes kids are better at finding ghosts than adults are."

Mrs. Beesley didn't invite Claire inside. But she hadn't closed her door yet, either.

"I'm also cheaper than most detectives," Claire went on. "Five bucks. That's all I charge. And if I don't solve your case, you don't have to pay me anything. Where are you going to find a better deal than that?" Claire smiled politely.

"Well," Mrs. Beesley said. "I certainly haven't been able to take care of this ghost problem myself. Most people don't even believe me when I say I have a ghost in my house. It couldn't hurt to try a child detective." She opened her screen door, and Claire stepped inside.

Kaz swam all around the inside of the bottle, trying to get a good look around Mrs. Beesley's house. He didn't have much of a view.

"Won't you sit down?" Mrs. Beesley led Claire to a flowered sofa.

"Don't forget to let me out," Kaz said. He was eager to find the ghost in Mrs. Beesley's house.

Claire dropped her detective bag on the sofa and plopped down beside it. "So," she said as she *sloooowly* twisted the top off her water bottle. "What makes you think that there's a ghost in your house?"

As soon as the top was off, Kaz shot out of the bottle. He expanded to full size right in front of Mrs. Beesley.

She couldn't see him.

"Hello? Mom? Dad?" Kaz called. "Are you here?"

"I hear it," Mrs. Beesley said. "I hear it moving around in the attic almost every day."

Claire reached into her bag and pulled out a notebook and a green pen. "What do you hear?" Claire asked, opening the notebook.

As he wafted around the living room, Kaz felt a strong breeze push him toward an open window.

"Aaaaah!" he shrieked, windmilling his arms and kicking his legs.

Claire jumped to her feet, but

somehow Kaz managed to escape the pull
of the wind and swim up along the ceiling.

"What?" Mrs. Beesley asked, turning
toward Kaz. "What's the matter?"

"Nothing," Claire said, sitting back
down.

There were a lot of open windows in
this house, Kaz noticed. Two in the living
room and one in the dining room. He
would have to be careful.

Claire picked up her notebook. "So, tell me about this ghost," she said to Mrs. Beesley as she crossed one leg over the other. "What do you hear?"

"Oh, all kinds of sounds. Rustling . . . thumping . . . scratching . . . something that sounds like marbles rolling all around the attic floor, even though I gave away the children's toys years ago."

There had been a marble in Kaz's old haunt. Even though the marble was solid, Little John could make it roll along the floor. It was one of his favorite things to do.

"Little John?" Kaz called as he swam into what appeared to be a kitchen. "Are you here?"

"Sometimes I hear someone crying, too," Mrs. Beesley went on as Kaz swam under the kitchen table.

"In the attic?" Claire asked.

"Yes. But then as soon as I open the attic door, all the noises stop."

Careful to avoid the windows, Kaz swam back through the dining room and living room. Little John was only six years old. If he was up in the attic by himself, he might cry. But Mrs. Beesley wouldn't be able to hear him. Not unless Little John was actually wailing.

"Have you ever seen the ghost?" Claire asked Mrs. Beesley.

"No," Mrs. Beesley admitted. "But sometimes when I'm sitting here in my chair, I feel a chill come over me."

Claire nodded and wrote that down.

Kaz swam down a dim hallway and into a sunny bedroom. This was not the sort of room ghosts liked to hang out in. It was too bright. But Kaz poked his

head in anyway. "Little John?" he called.

He didn't see Little John or any other ghosts.

There was a small bathroom across the hall from this bedroom. A shade hung over the window. It clunked against the window frame as it swayed in the breeze.

Kaz glided in and looked around.

No ghosts here, either.

There were two more doors at the end of the hall. One was open, the other was closed.

Mrs. Beesley and Claire were walking toward Kaz now.

"Hey, where are you guys going?" Kaz asked. He darted out of the way before Mrs. Beesley walked right through him.

Mrs. Beesley shivered. "Maybe I

should close some of these windows. It's feeling chilly in here."

Claire motioned with her head for Kaz to follow.

"Here we are. This is the attic," Mrs. Beesley said, reaching for the closed door. The door opened with a *creeeeeaaaak.*

Mrs. Beesley and Claire slowly clomped up the stairs. Kaz drifted behind them.

Now this is the kind of place a ghost might hang out, Kaz thought. He swam above Claire and Mrs. Beesley's heads and circled the attic. He saw lots of boxes up here. Boxes and old furniture. Much of it was covered in dust and cobwebs.

"Little John?" Kaz called. "Are you up here, Little John?"

Kaz felt a draft as he neared a window, but the window was closed. The whole place smelled a lot like his old haunt.

But there weren't any ghosts up here. It was just an old, dusty attic. Disappointment filled Kaz.

When Mrs. Beesley's back was turned, Claire mouthed to Kaz, "Any luck in the rest of this house?"

Kaz shook his head. "I don't think there are any ghosts here."

"Are you sure?" Claire whispered.

"Am I sure of what, dear?" Mrs. Beesley asked.

"Pretty sure," Kaz replied.

Claire smiled nervously at Mrs. Beesley. "Are you sure your ghost is still here?" She turned all around. "Because I don't see any ghosts."

"Just because you don't see one doesn't mean it's not here," Mrs. Beesley said. "Don't you have some sort of equipment to help you find ghosts? Like they do on TV."

"I only need my eyes," Claire said.

Mrs. Beesley looked doubtful.

"Woof! Woof!"

Kaz drifted over to the dusty window and peered into the Outside. He saw a dog barking at a squirrel.

But not just any dog. A ghost dog.

It was *Cosmo!*

CHAPTER 4

COME BACK, COSMO!

Cosmo?" Kaz called, staring out the window.

The ghost dog floated around a tree across the street. He looked up at Kaz and wagged his tail. Then the wind pushed him farther down the street.

Kaz didn't think. He just swam. . . across the attic and down the stairs.

"Kaz? Where are you going?" Claire asked as she raced down the stairs behind him.

"Kaz? Who's Kaz?" Mrs. Beesley called after Claire.

"Cosmo!" Kaz cried, paddling as hard and fast as he could . . . right over to the open living-room window.

"NO!" Claire yelled.

Too late. The wind *pullllled* Kaz through the window and into the Outside.

Oh no!

"Help! HELP!" Kaz screamed, struggling to get back inside. How could he have forgotten about the wind?

He felt Claire's hand pass through his foot, but she couldn't grab him or pull him back inside.

The wind carried Kaz away from Mrs. Beesley's house . . . and away from Claire.

Kaz soon heard footsteps pounding the sidewalk behind him. And Claire's voice: "Kaz! Come back!"

"I *caaaaaan't*," he called. "I can't swim against the wind."

Tears sprang to Kaz's eyes. "I'll miss you, Claire!" He waved good-bye.

All he could do was ride the wind and see where it took him next.

Up ahead, he saw a city bus turn a corner, pull over to the curb, and stop.

The door whooshed open, and Cosmo passed through a woman as she stepped off the bus.

The woman stopped for a second, looked all around her, and then kept on walking.

"Cosmo!" Kaz called. He had blown away from Claire, but maybe he could still catch up with his dog.

He saw Cosmo floating around inside the bus.

If the bus stayed parked for another thirty seconds . . . if the door stayed open . . . then Kaz would blow right into the bus, too.

He pumped his arms and legs. Faster . . . faster . . . faster . . . he was almost there.

But the door slammed shut a second and a half before Kaz reached it.

As the bus started to pull away, Kaz spotted an open window. He sailed inside.

"Woof! Woof!" Cosmo greeted him from the back window of the bus.

Kaz swam along the ceiling toward his dog. "Cosmo!" he cried as the dog leaped into his arms.

Cosmo licked Kaz all over and wagged his tail. Kaz buried his face in his dog's fur. "I'm so happy to see you, boy."

Then Kaz heard a voice outside. "STOP!" the voice called.

Kaz glanced out the back window and saw Claire running toward the bus. "STOP, BUS!" she yelled, waving her hands. Her detective bag swung from one hand and Kaz's empty bottle swung from the other.

Claire wasn't lost yet!

"Hurry, Claire!" Kaz yelled hopefully. "Hurry!"

But Claire couldn't run fast enough to catch a bus.

Kaz heard a bell ding. A man with a briefcase stood up and made his way to the front of the bus. The bus stopped to let him off.

"WAIT!" Claire yelled. She was starting to catch up, but the bus drove away again before she could reach it.

The bus traveled another block, then stopped to let an older woman get on.

Kaz glanced out the back window. Claire was running hard.

"Woof!" Cosmo wagged his tail as though he wanted her to hurry, too.

The older woman paid her bus fare. "You might want to wait for that girl," she said, pointing at Claire. "I think she's trying to catch the bus."

The driver waited.

Kaz waited.

And soon, an out-of-breath Claire hopped onto the bus.

"Claire!" Kaz cried. "I didn't think I'd ever see you again."

"Woof! Woof!" barked Cosmo.

Claire beamed at Kaz and his dog. She started down the aisle toward them, but the bus driver called her back.

"It costs fifty cents for kids to ride the bus," the driver said.

"Oh. Yeah." Claire reached into the front of her bag and pulled out some coins. "Where . . . does this bus . . . go?" she panted as she dropped her coins into the slot.

"Downtown."

"Okay. Good."

The bus started up again, and Claire staggered to the back of the bus where

Kaz and Cosmo were floating. She slid into the last seat.

Cosmo dived down and tried to lick Claire's neck. But because she was a solid, his tongue and part of his head passed through her.

"Claire, meet Cosmo," Kaz said.

"Hi, Cosmo." Claire giggled as Kaz's dog kept trying, and failing, to lick her.

The lady in the seat in front of them turned and gave Claire a funny look.

"Cosmo likes you," Kaz said.

"I like him, too," Claire said in a low voice. She shifted in her seat, then said, "You know, there are a lot of open windows on this bus. I think you and Cosmo should get back in the bottle. Otherwise you both might blow away again."

"Good idea," Kaz said. He sure didn't want to blow away.

The two teenagers in the seat across from Claire turned and raised their eyebrows as Claire opened her water bottle and held it for Kaz. The girl twirled a finger next to her ear, and the boy nodded.

"Why are those people looking at us?" Kaz asked. "Can they see me?" He waved at the teenagers, but they stared right through him.

"No," Claire said, barely moving her lips. "And they aren't looking at *us*. They're looking at *me*. They think I'm talking to myself."

The lady in front of them got up and moved to a seat closer to the front of the bus.

"Ohhh," Kaz said.

"So, maybe you should get in the

bottle and we should stop talking," Claire hissed. "Can your dog shrink, too?"

"I . . . don't know." Kaz assumed Cosmo could shrink like any other ghost. But he'd never actually seen Cosmo do it.

"Maybe if I do it first," Kaz said. He took a deep breath, shrank, and swam inside Claire's bottle. "Cosmo?" he called. "Come here, Cosmo!"

Cosmo stared curiously at Kaz inside the bottle. Then he sniffed the bottle, his nose covering the entire opening. He let out a frustrated doggy groan.

"Come on, boy." Kaz clapped his hands together. "You can do it."

Cosmo backed away from the bottle and groaned again. His eyes grew dark. His tail spun. Finally, he shrank to

Kaz's size and dog-paddled into the bottle.

"Good boy!" Kaz said, patting him on the back.

Claire put the lid on and held the bottle against her chest.

After a little while, the bus driver called, "Downtown. This is the last stop on this bus."

All the solids on the bus stood up. Claire grabbed her bag and water bottle and followed everyone else off the bus.

Kaz peered out through the side of the bottle. "Now what do we do?" he asked. "How will we ever get back to the library?"

"We'll walk back," Claire said. She pulled her phone out of her bag. "I'll look up how to do it." She stood in the middle of the sidewalk and slid

her finger all around the screen on her phone.

Kaz stared. He thought the phone was for talking to people who weren't there.

"Okay," Claire said, dropping the phone back into her bag. "I know how to get home now."

"What did you say to Mrs. Beesley when you left?" Kaz asked once Claire started walking. "Was she disappointed that we didn't find her ghost?"

"I told her I thought her ghost probably blew out the window," Claire said. "But Kaz, I think we *did* find her ghost. I think your dog, Cosmo, was her ghost! I think he was in her house and then he left or blew out."

"Hmm. Maybe," Kaz said, thinking about it. "I saw him barking at a squirrel

across the street from Mrs. Beesley's house. He used to do that all the time, back at our old haunt. We had to yell, 'No, Cosmo!' at him so he wouldn't pass through the wall and go chase the squirrels. But there wouldn't have been anyone to yell, 'No, Cosmo!' at him this morning."

Claire probably was right about Cosmo being Mrs. Beesley's ghost.

"Anyway," Claire continued, "I wrote down my cell-phone number and told her to call if the ghost comes back. And then I ran after you. I didn't even wait around for her to pay me. I was afraid that I wouldn't catch you if I didn't leave right away."

"I'm glad you did catch me," Kaz said.

"Me too," said Claire.

CHAPTER 5

MORE GHOST TROUBLE

hat the devil is *that*?" Beckett asked as Cosmo dog-paddled around the entryway of the library.

"My dog, Cosmo," Kaz said with a grin.

"Woof! Woof!" Cosmo barked.

"Okay." Beckett leaped out of the dog's way. "Maybe a better question is: Why is he *here*?"

Kaz didn't think that was a better question. He thought it was a strange

question. "Because *I'm* here," he said. "Cosmo is my dog, so he should be with me."

"We're going to bring all of Kaz's family here," Claire said as she dropped her detective bag by the door and kicked off her shoes. "Once we find them all."

"What?" Beckett exclaimed, his hat flying off his head. "No! You can't!"

"Why not?" Claire asked.

Beckett grabbed his hat and placed it firmly back on his head. "Because this is a library, not a hotel. There isn't room for Kaz's whole family." He darted out of the way as Cosmo dog-paddled past again.

"What are you talking about? There's plenty of room," Kaz said. The library was almost as big as his old haunt.

"Not in my private haunt, there isn't," Beckett said.

"No one said we'd all live there," Kaz said. Kaz had never even seen Beckett's secret room.

"Meow," called a soft voice from the stairs. Claire's cat, Thor, peeked between the slats of the railing.

"Uh-oh," Kaz said. He knew Thor didn't like *him* very much, and it looked as though Thor liked ghost dogs even less than he liked ghost boys.

But Cosmo wasn't afraid of Thor. "Woof! Woof!" Cosmo barked, lunging at the solid cat.

"MEOW!" Thor spun on his heels and bounded up the stairs.

Cosmo tore after Thor. He chased Claire's cat upstairs . . . then downstairs . . . then upstairs again . . . then back downstairs and into the children's room. Claire, Kaz, and Beckett raced after them.

Grandma Karen gasped as Thor leaped up onto her desk.

Cosmo nipped at Thor's tail, and Thor turned around and hissed. He batted his paw at Cosmo, but his paw passed through the ghost dog.

"Cosmo!" Kaz said at the same time Claire said, "Thor!"

"Good heavens!" Grandma Karen sank back against her chair. "What's the matter with that cat?"

Cosmo lunged for Thor. Thor jumped down and darted across the room. Cosmo stayed right on his tail. They ran from room to room until they couldn't run anymore. Then, they dropped to their bellies at opposite ends of the entryway.

"Well, that was entertaining," Beckett said with half a smile. "I changed my mind. The dog can stay."

* * * * * * * * * * * * * * *

"Woof! Woof!"

"MEOW!"

"Woof! Woof!"

"MEOW!"

Claire had a hard time sleeping that night. So did Grandma Karen.

A little after midnight, Kaz heard Grandma Karen's bedroom door creak open. "What's the trouble, Thor?" Grandma Karen whispered out in the hallway. "Where are you running off to in such a hurry?"

Claire threw her covers off and went to open her door.

"Did Thor wake you up, too?" Grandma Karen asked.

"Yeah, I guess," Claire replied with a yawn.

Grandma Karen shook her head. "That cat has been acting strange all day. It's like he sees something that isn't there."

Claire bit her lip.

Back in her bedroom, Claire told Kaz, "Your dog and my cat will make friends with each other eventually. They just need to get used to each other."

Kaz hoped she was right.

* * * * * * * * * * * * * * * * *

The next morning, all was quiet inside the library. Too quiet, Kaz and Claire agreed.

"Thor?" Claire called.

"Cosmo?" Kaz called.

Neither animal came when they were called.

"I wonder where they are," Claire said.

Kaz followed Claire into the kitchen. Claire opened a cabinet, pulled out a bag

of cat food, and shook it. The pellets inside rattled. "Thor?" she called again. "Are you hungry?"

Thor padded into the kitchen. "Meow?" he said, looking up at Claire.

But where was Cosmo?

Claire poured some cat food into a small bowl on the floor. Thor went over and gobbled it up.

Unfortunately, shaking a bag of food wouldn't work on Cosmo. Ghost dogs don't eat.

"Cosmo?" Kaz called, wafting through the living room. "Where are you, boy?" Cosmo was normally a well-behaved dog. It wasn't like him to not come when he was called.

Kaz poked his head into all the bedrooms. Cosmo didn't seem to be anywhere on the second floor.

"Maybe he's downstairs," Claire said. "I'll help you look."

Kaz and Claire searched the fiction room.

No Cosmo.

They searched the nonfiction room.

No Cosmo.

While they were searching the children's room, a boy looked up from the book he was reading. It was that redheaded boy who lived next door to Mrs. Beesley.

"Hey, aren't you the girl who was at my neighbor's house yesterday?" the boy asked. He had lots of dots on his face. "What's your name?"

"Claire."

Kaz glanced nervously at the fan in the ceiling. Fans were like the Outside wind, except they blew you around in circles and made you sick.

"I'm Eli," the boy said. "Why were you at Mrs. Beesley's house? Are you related to her or something?"

"No. She hired me to do a job," Claire said.

"What job?" Eli asked.

Claire hesitated for a second. Then she said, "She hired me to find her ghost."

Eli burst out laughing.

"What?" Claire frowned. "What's so funny?"

"Did you find a ghost?" Eli asked, still laughing.

Claire put her hand on her hip. "As a matter of fact, I did."

"Really?" Eli's eyebrow shot up. "You found a ghost at her house? A real, live ghost?"

Claire shrugged. "I solved her problem. I don't expect you to understand."

"I bet you didn't. Solve her problem, I mean," Eli said. "Mrs. Beesley's problems are never solved. Whenever she hires me to do something, she makes me come back ten times and do it all over again." He grinned. "But I always get even."

"What do you mean?" Claire asked.

This conversation with Eli wasn't helping them find Cosmo, so Kaz decided to keep looking by himself.

There was still one room he and

Claire hadn't searched: the craft room.

But Cosmo wasn't in there, either. He didn't seem to be anywhere in the library.

So where was he?

Kaz swallowed hard. If Cosmo wasn't anywhere inside the library, then . . . he must be *outside* the library.

Maybe when he and Thor had been chasing each other during the night, Cosmo had accidentally passed through the wall into the Outside. That was exactly what happened to Kaz's brother Finn that horrible day when he, Kaz, and Little John had been playing Keep Away back at their old haunt.

Kaz floated back to the main hallway and over to a big bay window. He peered into the Outside, but he didn't see Cosmo. Kaz wasn't surprised. By now, the wind would've blown Cosmo away.

"That Eli isn't very nice," Claire said, joining Kaz at the window. "He told me about all these tricks he's played on Mrs. Beesley."

"What kind of tricks?" Kaz asked.

"Ringing her doorbell and running

away," Claire said. "Putting fake dog poop on her porch and then taking it away when she goes to get something to clean it up. Stuff like that."

"Why would he do that?" Kaz asked.

Claire shrugged. "Because whenever

he rakes leaves for her or mows her lawn, she makes him come back and do a better job. He likes to play tricks on her to get even."

All of a sudden, a catchy tune sounded from Claire's detective bag.

"Hey, that's my phone," Claire said. She pulled the phone out of her bag and put it to her ear. "Hello? Uh huh . . . uh huh . . ." Claire glanced at Kaz. "Really!" she said. "Yeah. I'll be right over." She put the telephone back in her bag and turned to Kaz. "That was Mrs. Beesley," she said. "Her ghost is back! I wonder if Cosmo got out of the library and went back to Mrs. Beesley's house."

Kaz's heart gave a leap. Was that possible?

CHAPTER 6

TRAPPED!

"Where are you going, dear?" Grandma Karen asked as Claire reached for the doorknob. "And why are you taking an empty water bottle with you?"

Claire glanced down at Kaz, who was safe inside the "empty" water bottle. She let out a small laugh. "Oh, did I forget to fill it? I better go do that."

Claire ran up the stairs two at a time, the bottle swinging at her side. Once she

and Kaz were alone in the kitchen, she untwisted the lid on the bottle.

"Is it okay to put some water in there with you?" Claire asked. "I don't want my grandma to get suspicious."

Kaz knew what water was. It was like rain that solids could turn on and off inside their haunts.

"Yes," Kaz said. "But leave some room for me to swim above the water."

Kaz had seen Claire put water into a bowl for Thor before, but he had no idea how *hard* and *fast* it came out of the faucet.

"Aaaaaaaah!" he shrieked as the water poured down on him inside the bottle.

Claire yanked the bottle away from the stream of water. "What? What's the matter?" she asked.

Kaz shook himself. "I didn't know the water was going to fall so hard. Or that it would pass through me."

"Sorry!" Claire said. "I'll turn it down." She moved a knob, and the water came out much slower.

"Who are you talking to, Claire?" Grandma Karen asked from the doorway.

Claire jumped. "No one. Just myself."

Kaz hovered near the side of the bottle as water rose below him.

Grandma Karen stared hard at the water bottle. She stared so hard that for a second Kaz wondered if she could see him. But then Grandma Karen turned her attention to Claire. "You've been talking to yourself a lot lately," she said.

Claire shrugged. "I like to talk to myself."

Grandma Karen smiled. "I did, too, when I was your age," she said. "So, where are you off to?"

"Um . . . a lady asked me to come help her do some stuff," Claire said as she turned off the water.

"What lady?" Grandma Karen asked.

Claire put the top back on her bottle. It was only about half full of water. "Her name is Mrs. Beesley."

Grandma Karen's face brightened. "Do you mean Victoria Beesley who lives over on Forest Street?"

"Yes," Claire said carefully.

"I know Victoria. She comes into the library from time to time. It's nice of you to help her out."

"So it's okay if I go?" Claire asked.

"Yes," Grandma Karen said. "As long as you're home in time for dinner."

* * * * * * * * * * * * * * * *

"Cosmo?" Kaz called as he swam around inside Mrs. Beesley's house. He had to be careful because, once again, there were a lot of open windows. "Cosmo, are you here?"

Claire sat on the sofa next to Mrs. Beesley. "How do you know the ghost is back?" Claire asked as she opened her notebook and dropped her detective bag at her feet.

"I heard those sounds again," Mrs. Beesley said. "Crying . . . thumping . . . marbles rolling across the ceiling. Someone's up there. I can feel him when I'm up there, even if I can't see him."

All of a sudden, they heard a loud CRASH! above their heads. And then footsteps scurrying across the ceiling.

"What's that noise?" Claire asked, looking up.

"It's the ghost!" Mrs. Beesley said as she rose to her feet. "Let's see if we can catch him."

Kaz followed Claire and Mrs. Beesley up the attic stairs. But something was bothering him: Ghosts don't walk with their feet on the floor, so they don't make footsteps.

When they reached the top of the stairs, Kaz, Claire, and Mrs. Beesley all looked around. Kaz didn't see any ghosts. He didn't see any solids, either. All he saw was a broken lamp lying on the floor.

"Oh no," Mrs. Beesley moaned when she noticed the lamp. She hurried over.

"This was my mother's lamp," she said, staring down at the pieces. She shook her head sadly. "I came across it when I was sorting through some boxes the other day. I don't know why I didn't put it away."

"I'm sorry," Claire said.

Mrs. Beesley's jaw tightened. "Well, lamps don't break by themselves," she said. "And I don't see anyone else up here.

It must have been a ghost who broke
that lamp, don't you think?"

"Maybe," Claire said with a sideways
glance at Kaz.

While Claire and Mrs. Beesley
gathered up the broken pieces, Kaz
drifted around the attic.

"Cosmo!" he hissed, turning all
around. "Are you up here? Did you

knock that lamp on the floor?" He had seen his dog move solid objects back in their old haunt. Cosmo *maybe* could move a lamp.

But if Cosmo was up there, he was hiding.

Kaz checked under a bed . . . behind a pile of boxes . . . under two chairs. No Cosmo.

He checked behind a bookshelf . . . behind another pile of boxes. Still no Cosmo.

As he floated near the window, Kaz felt the pull of the wind. *That's odd*, he thought . . . until he noticed that the window was open!

Kaz was pretty sure that window was closed yesterday. But before he could ask Claire about it, the downstairs attic door slammed shut.

CHAPTER 7

ESCAPE

Claire tramped down the stairs and tried the door. "Uh-oh," she said, glancing up at Kaz and Mrs. Beesley. "We're locked in here."

"What?" Mrs. Beesley cried. "That door is never locked." Holding tight to the railing, she slowly made her way down the stairs and tried the door herself.

It was indeed locked.

"You have a key, don't you?" asked Claire.

"Yes," Mrs. Beesley said. "But . . . it's in the lock. On the other side of the door. Do you have a cell phone? We could call one of my neighbors and ask them to come over and unlock the door."

"I do," Claire said. "But it's in my bag. And I left my bag in the living room."

"What are we going to do?" Mrs. Beesley moaned.

A noise in the Outside caught Kaz's attention. He knew that window was open, so he didn't want to get too close. But he was close enough to catch a glimpse of that neighbor boy, Eli, running across Mrs. Beesley's yard toward his own yard.

"Claire! Claire!" Kaz cried. "Come quick!"

Claire clomped back up the stairs.

"Look outside," Kaz said, backing away from the window.

Claire strode over to the window. "Hey, this window is open," she called to Mrs. Beesley.

"Yes," Mrs. Beesley said from halfway up the stairs. "It smelled musty up here, so I opened it this morning."

"Do you see Eli?" Kaz asked Claire, stretching the top part of his body a

little bit closer, but not *too* close, to the window. "I saw him running over to his own yard from Mrs. Beesley's yard. Could he be Mrs. Beesley's ghost? Could he have climbed that tree out there and sneaked into the attic? Could he have made all those noises, and broken the lamp, and locked us in here to play another trick on Mrs. Beesley?"

"I don't know, but I'm going to find out," Claire said.

Kaz darted out of Claire's way.

"What are you going to find out, dear?" Mrs. Beesley asked.

Claire raised the window as high as it would go and swung her leg over the windowsill.

Mrs. Beesley's eyes widened. "What are you doing?" she cried as Claire climbed out onto the roof.

"I'm going to climb down that tree and find out what's going on. Then I'm going to come back through your front door and open the attic door."

Mrs. Beesley gasped. "B-but you could fall!"

"I'll be okay," Claire said. Holding her arms out to the sides for balance, she *sloooowly* walked across the roof.

Mrs. Beesley stood at the window and wrung her hands nervously. She didn't take her eyes off Claire.

Kaz was just as worried as Mrs. Beesley was. What if Claire slipped and fell? What if she fell all the way to the ground? Solids weren't like ghosts. They could get hurt. Really badly.

Mrs. Beesley gasped again as Claire reached for the tree branch that ran alongside the roof.

Kaz closed his eyes. He couldn't bear to watch. But he couldn't bear to *not* watch, either. He opened one eye and watched Claire crawl along the tree branch.

Careful not to get too close to the window, Kaz watched Claire climb down the branches as though they were stairs. Soon she disappeared from Kaz's view.

Kaz sailed across the attic and down along the stairs. There was no carpet here like there was on the second floor

of the library, so when he reached the closed door, he took a deep breath, made himself as flat as a piece of paper, and swam under the door. He needed to get someplace where he could see Claire.

He started to go inside one of the bedrooms, but the window was wide open. Kaz could feel the pull of the Outside, so he backed away.

He tried the next bedroom. The window in this room was open only a

crack. He swam to the top of the window and looked outside. He saw Claire talking to Eli, the boy next door.

Whew. Claire was safe.

Claire and Eli didn't talk for long. After a couple of minutes, she broke away and ran toward Mrs. Beesley's house. Kaz couldn't wait to hear what she had found out.

He swam to the living room. The windows in there were open, too, but it was a larger room, so he wasn't as likely to get pulled into the Outside. Not unless he got too close to a window. He watched as the knob on the front door turned.

But the door didn't open.

"That door's locked, too?" Kaz cried.

"No problem," Claire said from outside. "The window's open." She climbed in through the window, then closed the window behind her.

Kaz was so happy to see Claire that he wanted to hug her. He did it very carefully, so he didn't pass through.

"Aw," Claire said. "Were you worried about me, Kaz?"

"Sort of," Kaz admitted. "So? Is Eli the ghost?"

"He says he's not," Claire said, grabbing her bag. "He said he came over to Mrs. Beesley's yard to get his ball and then he left."

"So how did the attic door slam shut?" Kaz asked.

"I don't know." Claire turned toward the open dining-room window. The curtains around it fluttered in the breeze. "Maybe the wind blew it closed?"

"Maybe," Kaz said. There certainly wasn't anyone else, ghost or solid, in the house who could've slammed it shut.

"Or maybe Eli lied," Claire said.

All of a sudden, there was a scream from the attic.

Claire ran and Kaz swam to the attic door. "Mrs. Beesley?" Claire cried. "Are you okay?"

"Claire? Is that you? Hurry and open this door," Mrs. Beesley demanded. "The ghost is back, and it's after me!"

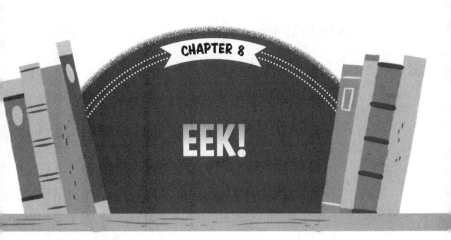

CHAPTER 8

EEK!

Claire wiggled the key in the lock, and the attic door popped open. Mrs. Beesley hurried out and quickly slammed the door closed behind her.

"Did you see the ghost this time?" Claire asked.

"No." Mrs. Beesley shook her head, her back pressed firmly against the door. "But I heard it. I think that ghost is angry with us for disturbing it."

"Why do you think it's angry?" Claire asked.

"Because it was making a lot of noise, more than before, like it was trying to scare me away," Mrs. Beesley said with a shiver. Her face had grown very pale.

"I didn't hear any noise after you left the attic," Kaz told Claire. "But I was swimming around down here looking for you."

"What did you hear?" Claire asked.

"Thumping, scratching, and a sort of *reH-reH-REE* noise," Mrs. Beesley replied.

ReH-reH-REE? "Like a dog?" Kaz asked, though *reH-reH-REE* wasn't really a sound Cosmo made.

"Did it sound like a dog?" Claire asked.

"No," Mrs. Beesley said. "It sounded like a ghost!"

"*ReH-reH-REE* doesn't sound like a
ghost wail at all," Kaz said.

"Do you want me to go check it
out?" Claire asked.

"No!" Mrs. Beesley shook her head.
"Whatever is up there, it's too much for
the two of us to handle by ourselves. I
think I should call someone." She strode
down the hall.

Claire followed. "Who?" she asked as Mrs. Beesley picked up her phone. "Who are you going to call?"

"I-I don't know," Mrs. Beesley said. She put the phone down and sank into her chair. "Who would believe that I've got a ghost in my attic? None of my neighbors believe me. They all think I'm crazy."

Claire touched Mrs. Beesley's arm. "I believe you," she said.

"You do?" Kaz gaped at Claire. "You really think there's a ghost in Mrs. Beesley's attic?" Kaz wasn't so sure.

"Please, let me go up and look around one more time," Claire begged. "If there's really a ghost in your attic, I can talk to him and see what he wants."

"I don't know." Mrs. Beesley

scratched her head. "I don't think it's a good idea."

"I really don't think he wants to hurt anyone," Claire said. "Most ghosts don't."

"Well . . . ," Mrs. Beesley said. "I don't think I want to go back up there. But if you really want to look around one more time, you have my permission. Let's make sure the attic door is propped open this time, though. Okay?"

"Okay," Claire said.

She and Mrs. Beesley headed back down the hall. Claire opened the attic door, and Mrs. Beesley set a box in front of the door to hold it open.

Kaz drifted behind Claire as she marched up the attic stairs. When they reached the top, they stopped and listened.

All they heard was a gentle breeze through the leaves outside the open window.

Claire closed the window. They listened some more.

The attic was quiet.

"I don't think there are any ghosts up here," Kaz said, breaking the silence.

"I don't, either," Claire admitted. "But we're detectives, remember?"

"What does that mean?" Kaz asked. When Claire said they should start a

detective agency to find his family, Kaz thought that meant they would simply go over to someone's house and look for ghosts. He didn't know how to be a real detective like Claire's parents.

Did Claire?

Claire sat down on an old trunk. "All I know is that Mrs. Beesley hired us to do a job," she said. "Ghost or not, she hired us to find whatever is haunting her attic. So that's what I think we should do."

"Okay," Kaz said. "How do we do that?"

"Maybe we should start by making a list of all the clues we've found so far," Claire said. She reached into her detective bag and pulled out her notebook and green pen. "Let's make a list of everything Mrs. Beesley said. Everything that makes her think there's a ghost in her house."

"She heard crying, scratching, and a *reH-reH-REE* sound," Kaz said. "But that doesn't sound like any ghost I know."

"We should write it down, anyway," Claire said.

"She also said she heard marbles rolling on the floor," Kaz went on. "But I don't see any marbles. Plus she gave her kids' toys away a long time ago."

Claire nodded as she wrote. "The noises usually stop when Mrs. Beesley comes up to the attic," she said. "But they didn't stop when she was up here by herself a little while ago. They got louder. Like someone was trying to scare her away."

"She's never seen a ghost in her house," Kaz said. "Is that a clue? Because she would only see a ghost if the ghost was glowing, you know."

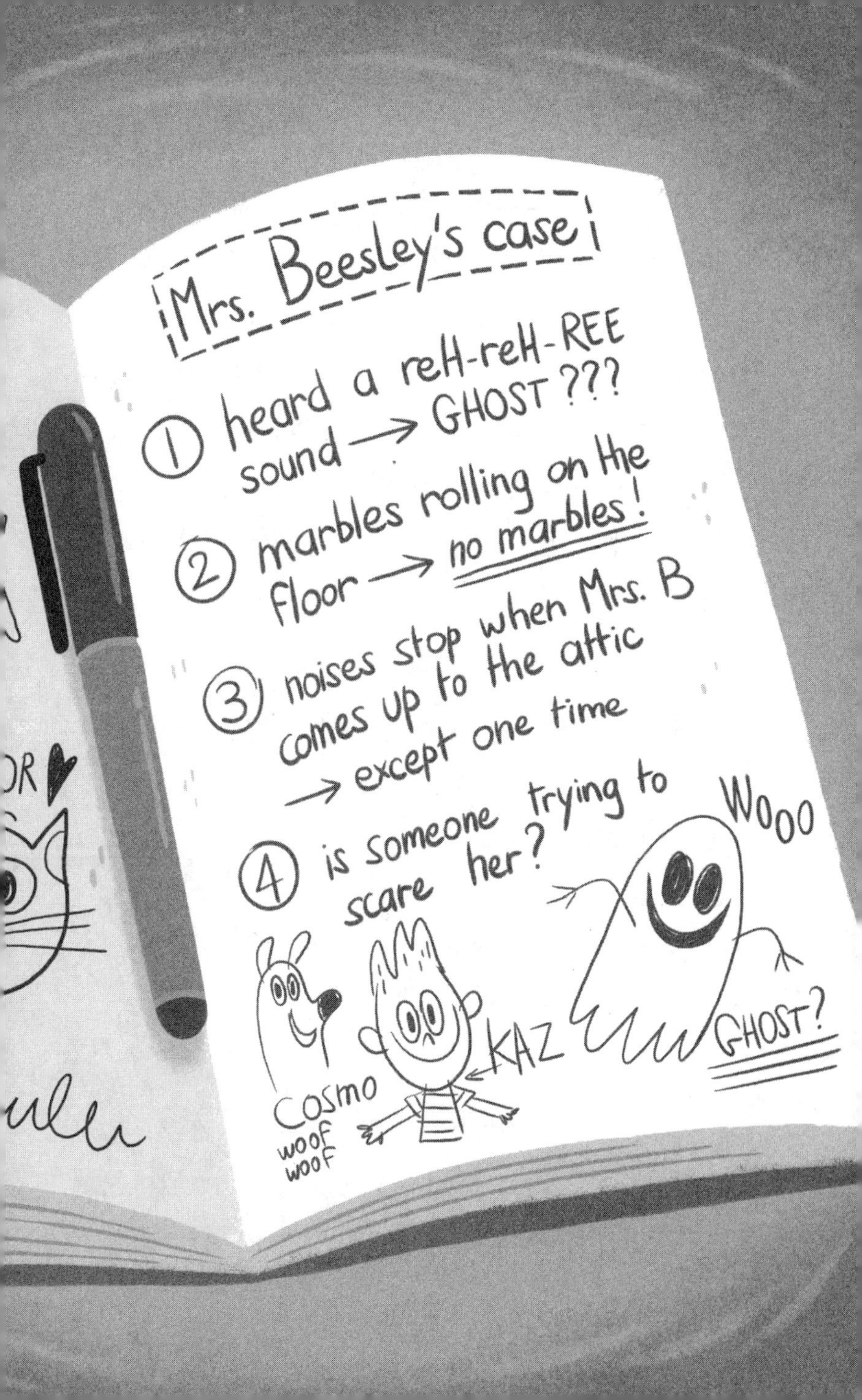
Mrs. Beesley's case
① heard a reH-reH-REE sound → GHOST ???
② marbles rolling on the floor → no marbles!
③ noises stop when Mrs. B comes up to the attic → except one time
④ is someone trying to scare her?
Wooo
COSMO
woof woof
KAZ
GHOST?
OR

"I know," Claire said, writing it down. "It could be a clue. The fact that *we* haven't seen any ghosts here is a clue, too. Because we *can* see them, even when they're not glowing. The only ghost we've seen around here is your dog, Cosmo. But we never saw him inside the house."

Kaz's heart ached at the mention of his dog.

"He could've been inside when we weren't looking," Kaz said. "He's strong for a ghost dog. He could've closed the attic door. He could've knocked the lamp off that dresser. He could've rolled things around the attic and made all kinds of noises."

Claire wrote all that down.

"But he wouldn't have made any footsteps," Kaz said. "We heard footsteps."

Claire nodded. "Anything else? We

should write down everything. Because even if we don't think it's a clue, it could still be important."

Kaz thought some more. "Mrs. Beesley said she sometimes feels a chill in the air."

"Right," Claire said. "And you saw Eli running across the yard right after the attic door slammed shut."

"But Mrs. Beesley heard 'ghost noises' while you were talking to Eli, so he couldn't have been the one making those noises," Kaz said.

"So, does Mrs. Beesley have a ghost or not?" Claire asked, tapping her pen against her chin.

"Maybe she's just a crazy person, like her neighbors and your mom and dad said," Kaz suggested.

"Because she says she has a ghost in her house?" Claire asked. "People think

I'm weird if I let them know I see ghosts. Do you think I'm weird, Kaz?"

"No," said Kaz right away. He felt bad for even suggesting that Mrs. Beesley might be crazy.

"Let's see if the answer is in the clues," Claire said, turning back to her notebook.

Kaz hovered over Claire's shoulder and watched her write YES next to each clue that sounded ghostlike, NO next to clues that did *not* sound ghostlike, and MAYBE next to clues that could go either way. When she finished she circled one MAYBE.

Kaz sighed. "We aren't any closer to solving this case now than we were before we made that list."

"ReH-reH-REE!"

Kaz and Claire turned to each other. "What was *that?*" Kaz asked.

CHAPTER 9

GHOSTS UNCOVERED

ReH-reH-REE! ReH-reH-REE!"

The noise was coming from under a bed in the corner of the attic.

"Is *that* the noise Mrs. Beesley heard?" Claire asked, wrinkling her nose. "You're right. That doesn't sound like a ghost at all."

"Actually, Little John sort of sounds like that when he laughs," Kaz said. Could Little John be hiding up there somewhere? Could *he* be Mrs. Beesley's ghost?

Kaz dived down and swam under the bed. It was dark under there, but Kaz could still see pretty well.

"Is there anything under there?" Claire asked.

Clumps of dust. Acorns. A pencil. But no ghosts.

"ReH-reH-REE!"

Kaz spun around. "Little John?"

"ReH-reH-REE!"

The noise wasn't just coming from under this bed. It was coming from a hole in a floorboard . . . under the bed.

Kaz stared into the hole, but it was too dark to see anything. So he shrunk down as small as he could and dived into the hole.

He counted one . . . two . . . three . . . four . . . five HUGE pairs of eyes staring at him.

"Aaaaaaahhhhhh!" he screamed as he shot out of the hole and up from under the bed.

"What?" Claire leaped out of Kaz's way as he expanded to his normal size. "What's the matter? Did you find Mrs. Beesley's ghost?"

"Yes," Kaz said, his heart pounding like crazy. "But they're not ghosts. They're solids!"

"*They're?*" Claire said. "You mean there's more than one?"

Kaz nodded.

"What are they?"

"I don't know," Kaz said. "All I know is they're small . . . and furry . . . and they have really big, scary eyes. There are a whole bunch of them under that bed!"

Claire knelt down and peered under the bed.

"No, no," Kaz said. He knew Claire would never see them like that. "You have to crawl under there to see them. You might even have to move the bed. They're in a hole in the floor."

Claire stood up, grabbed hold of the edge of the bed, and pulled. Kaz backed away.

"There," he said, pointing at the hole. "They're in there."

Claire opened her bag and took out a flashlight. She shone its light in the hole. "I don't see them," she said. She dropped to her knees and looked closer.

"Oh," she said, rocking back onto her heels. "Now I see."

Claire smiled at Kaz. "So . . . the chill in the air that Mrs. Beesley felt and the slammed door were probably caused by the wind from the open window. And

Eli really did come over to get his ball like he said. But the 'marbles,' the crying, the *reH-reH-REE* sound, the rustling, the thumping, the scratching, the footsteps, the broken lamp—all of that was caused by our 'ghosts' that aren't really ghosts."

Kaz was impressed. Claire sounded like a real detective.

Claire swept the beam of her flashlight across the lamp cord . . . a pile of strange black pellets . . . and some acorns, then moved the flashlight back to the black pellets.

"In fact," Claire said, walking over to the pellets. "I think we missed some clues. I bet our 'ghosts' left these behind."

"How did the 'ghosts' even get in here?" Kaz asked. "Did they come in through the window?"

"I don't think so," Claire said as she walked along the far wall of the attic. "Mrs. Beesley said she just opened that window this morning. I think these guys have been here for a while. They must've come in a different way."

Claire scanned the floor, the ceiling, and the wall in between.

"Aha!" she said, raising her eyes to

the vent above the window. "Look up there." She pointed.

Kaz swam up and took a closer look at the vent. He remembered feeling a draft when he swam by there yesterday. Now he knew why: Some of the slats on the vent were bent and broken.

Claire went to the attic stairs. "Mrs. Beesley?" she called down. "I found your ghosts."

"Ghosts?" Mrs. Beesley appeared at the foot of the stairs. "You mean there's more than one?"

"Yes. It's a mom and four babies," Claire said. "But they're not really ghosts."

Mrs. Beesley looked worried. "What are they, then?" she asked.

Claire smiled. "Come on up and see for yourself."

CHAPTER 10

CASE CLOSED

laire led Mrs. Beesley over to the floorboard with the hole and turned on the flashlight.

Mrs. Beesley squinted. "Squirrels?" she said. "Those are my ghosts?"

Claire nodded. "I think the mother came in over there. See?" She pointed to the attic vent. "Then she found this hole and made a nest in it for her babies."

"ReH-reH-REE!"

Mrs. Beesley tipped her head toward the noise. "That's the sound I heard earlier. That, and the crying, and the marbles rolling."

"I think the babies make a crying sound when the mother is away," Claire told Mrs. Beesley. "And the marble sound was probably rolling acorns."

"Imagine that," Mrs. Beesley said, shaking her head. "I can't thank you

enough for solving this mystery for me."

So the case was closed. But Cosmo was still lost.

"Let's go downstairs. I'll get my purse so I can pay you," Mrs. Beesley said.

Claire grinned at Kaz as she tramped down the stairs after Mrs. Beesley. "We're going to get paid!" she mouthed. "Isn't that great?"

Kaz didn't care about getting paid. Ghosts had no use for money. He wanted to find his dog. That was the whole reason he came back to Mrs. Beesley's house today. To find Cosmo.

But he had to face facts: Cosmo was gone. Probably for good.

"Thank you for believing me when I said I had a ghost in my attic," Mrs. Beesley said as she placed several bills in Claire's hand.

"I know what it feels like when people don't believe you," Claire said. "Thank you for the money."

She opened her bottle, and Kaz swam inside. It was time to go back to the library.

* * * * * * * * * * * * * * * * *

"Cosmo could still be hiding somewhere in here," Claire said to Kaz as she opened the front door and stepped inside the library entryway.

"I doubt it," Kaz grumbled.

"Claire? Is that you?" Grandma Karen called from the craft room.

"Yes," Claire said. She opened the bottle, and Kaz swam out.

"Would you come in here, please? I'd like to talk to you," Grandma Karen said.

Claire headed for the craft room. Kaz drifted behind.

"Woof! Woof!"

Kaz could hardly believe his eyes. Grandma Karen was reading at the table. And there, at her feet, was his dog.

"Cosmo!" he cried. "Where have you been, boy?"

Cosmo swam up and licked Kaz's face.

Had Cosmo been there at the library all along? *Where?*

Grandma Karen looked up from her book. "I think I know why Thor was behaving so strangely yesterday," she said to Claire in a funny voice.

"Oh?" Claire said. Kaz could tell she was trying to "act normal," like she didn't see Kaz or Cosmo.

"Tell me, Claire," Grandma Karen said. "Do you see a ghost dog anywhere in this room?"

"WHAT?" Claire's voice went high.

Grandma Karen smiled. She dropped her hand over the arm of the chair and made a kissing sound. "Here, doggie, doggie!"

Cosmo started to GLOW.

"Oh no," Kaz said, slapping his hand to his forehead.

Tail wagging, Cosmo broke away from Kaz and scampered over to Grandma Karen.

"*Now* do you see him?" Grandma Karen asked as she scratched Cosmo's ears. Her

hand passed through his head, but he didn't seem to mind.

Claire looked around nervously. "Grandma," she hissed. "*Everyone* can see him now."

"Relax, dear," Grandma Karen said. "There's no one here but us."

Well . . . and me, thought Kaz.

Grandma Karen stopped scratching Cosmo's ears, and he stopped glowing.

"You can still see this little dog, can't you?" Grandma Karen said to Claire.

Claire bit her lip and nodded. "How did you know?"

"Well, the fact that you talk to yourself so often was a clue. And I just got off the phone with Victoria Beesley. She called to tell me what a help you were in finding her 'ghost.'"

Kaz and Claire exchanged a look. They hadn't expected their customers to call Claire's grandma. Or worse: her parents.

"Also," Grandma Karen said, leaning toward Claire. "Can I let you in on a little secret?"

"Sure," Claire said.

"When I was your age, I could see ghosts."

"What? Really?" Claire stared wide-eyed.

Grandma Karen nodded.

Claire tilted her head. "You mean you could see them when you were a kid, but you can't anymore?"

"Not unless they're glowing."

"You know about glowing?" Claire asked. Her eyes grew even wider.

"Yes." Grandma Karen smiled.

Claire pulled out a chair and sat down next to her grandma. "Tell me about the ghosts you saw when you were a kid."

"Well, it started when I was nine, like you. One day I couldn't see them; the next day I could. There were two of them at my school. And there was one at my friend JoAnn's house. I don't even remember all the ghosts I knew as a child. Most of them were very kind."

Of course they were, Kaz thought.

"They kept me from feeling lonely,"

Grandma Karen went on. "But then something happened when I got older, and I couldn't see them anymore."

"What happened?" Claire asked.

"I don't know."

Claire bit her lip. "So it could happen to me, too. I might not always be able to see ghosts."

"Well, I can't say for sure. But probably," Grandma Karen said gently.

Kaz felt a little stab in his heart. Claire was his friend. He'd never had a friend before. But there could come a day when she wouldn't be able to see him. Not unless he learned to glow!

"I miss the ghosts," Grandma Karen said with a wistful smile. "That's why I like to pretend the library is haunted. I like to think there could still be ghosts floating around, keeping an eye on

things. But then this morning, I heard Thor meowing really loudly. I came to see what all the trouble was, and I found him sitting in the doorway over there like he was afraid to come in. Then I saw this ghost dog come scampering through that wall." She pointed at the wall of books in the back of the room.

"Through that wall right there?" Kaz asked, confused.

Beckett poked his face through the wall of books. "Yeah, yeah. I took pity on the poor animal and invited him to join me back here," Beckett said. "He keeps that cat away."

"Woof! Woof!" Cosmo barked, then darted through the wall. Beckett disappeared then, too.

Kaz grinned. He wouldn't have guessed Beckett was an animal lover.

"I only saw the dog for a little bit," Grandma Karen continued, "because he stopped glowing. But I knew he was still here. I could tell by the way Thor was carrying on."

"I have news for you, Grandma," Claire said. "There isn't just a ghost dog in this library. There are ghost *people* here, too."

"There are?" Grandma Karen leaned forward in her chair.

"Yes. There's a ghost man named Beckett. He's kind of boring. There's also a ghost boy named Kaz. He's my friend. He just got here a few weeks ago. And his dog, Cosmo, just got here yesterday."

"Beckett . . . Kaz . . . and Cosmo," Grandma Karen said like she was trying to remember all their names.

Claire told her grandma about Kaz's

old haunt getting torn down and his family all blowing away. Then she told about how she and Kaz had found Cosmo, lost him, and now found him again.

"Kaz must be happy to have his dog back," Grandma Karen said. "We have to help him find the rest of his family."

"I know," Claire said. "That's why he and I started a detective agency. We're C & K Ghost Detectives. But we have to be careful because Mom and Dad don't want me to talk about ghosts, and they don't want me to be a detective. They just want me to be normal."

"*Pfft.*" Grandma Karen waved her hand. "What's normal? You have a gift—"

"A gift?" Claire said. "Seeing ghosts is a gift?"

"Well, yes. But that's not what I

meant." Grandma Claire touched Claire's hair. "You have a good heart. That's your gift. You want to help your friend, even if it means doing something your parents asked you not to do. Let me help you with your parents."

"Would you do that?" Claire asked.

"Of course," Grandma Karen said. "Is Kaz here right now?"

"Yes. But he can't glow, so you won't be able to see him."

"Where is he?" Grandma Karen looked around. "Is he in that water bottle? Is that why you've been carrying it with you everywhere?"

"Yes," Claire admitted. "So Kaz can go outside with me and not blow away. But he's not in there right now. He's over there." She pointed to where Kaz was floating in the room.

Grandma Karen got up from her chair and walked over to Kaz. "Hello, Kaz," she said, holding out her hand. "I'm Karen."

"Nice to meet you," Kaz said. But he didn't take Grandma Karen's hand.

"He won't shake your hand," Claire said. "He doesn't like the way it feels when a solid hand passes through his. But he did say, 'Nice to meet you.'"

"It's nice to meet you, too, Kaz," Grandma Karen said.

Funny—Kaz's family had always told him to beware of solids. But so far, every solid—er, *person* who wasn't a ghost—that he'd met had been nothing but kind to him. He wished he could tell his family that. Maybe one day he'd be able to. Maybe, with Claire and Grandma Karen's help, Kaz would find the rest of his family again.

He hoped so.

But if not, Kaz knew he could be happy here with Claire and Grandma Karen for a long, long, long time. Maybe even forever.